For Florrie   S.W.

Text by Elena Pasquali
Illustrations copyright © 2011 Sophie Windham
This edition copyright © 2011 Lion Hudson

A Lion Children's Book
an imprint of
Lion Hudson plc
Wilkinson House, Jordan Hill Road,
Oxford OX2 8DR, England
www.lionhudson.com
Paperback ISBN 978 0 7459 6170 5
Hardback ISBN 978 0 7459 6289 4

First UK edition 2011
1 3 5 7 9 10 8 6 4 2 0
First US edition 2011
1 3 5 7 9 10 8 6 4 2 0

A catalogue record for this book is available
from the British Library

Typeset in 16/22 Baskerville Old Face
Printed in China January 2011 (manufacturer LH06)

Distributed by:
UK: Marston Book Services Ltd, PO Box 269, Abingdon, Oxon OX14 4YN
USA: Trafalgar Square Publishing, 814 N Franklin Street, Chicago, IL 60610
USA Christian Market: Kregel Publications, PO Box 2607, Grand Rapids, MI 49501

THE THREE TREES

A Traditional Folktale

Elena Pasquali ✽ Sophie Windham

LION
CHILDREN'S

Long ago, on a hillside, stood three trees.
In the spring, their roots drank in the cool raindrops
that trickled through the soil.

In the summer, they unfolded their leaves to the sun.
In the autumn, strong winds tousled their branches.
In winter, they rested under the sparkling snow.

Under the cold night sky that glittered with stars, they dreamed their dreams.

"Mine," said the first tree, "is of riches. I want to be made into a beautiful chest that will hold the finest treasure."

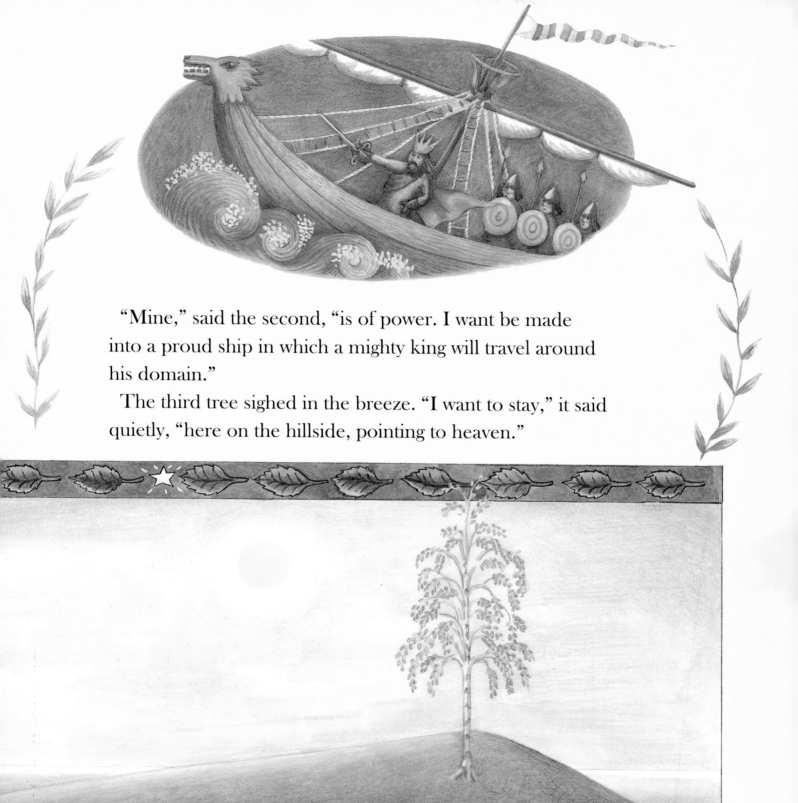

"Mine," said the second, "is of power. I want be made into a proud ship in which a mighty king will travel around his domain."

The third tree sighed in the breeze. "I want to stay," it said quietly, "here on the hillside, pointing to heaven."

Many years went by, and the trees grew tall and strong.

One day, three woodcutters climbed the hill, each with an axe in his hand.

"I am ready for riches," said the first tree as it fell.

"I bow to the king," said the second.

But the third tree shed its fragile leaves like tears. "Now my dream is over," it wept as it fell to the ground.

A carpenter took the wood from the first tree, sawed it into planks,
and then joined them.

It was a box he made – and he made it well – but it was not a chest.
It was a sturdy trough.

An innkeeper came and carted it away. Every evening, he filled it with hay for the weary creatures that his guests brought to his stable.

"Such a humble life," sighed the tree. "Such a poor and dismal place."

One night, the innkeeper led the animals aside, and a man and a woman took shelter in the stable.

Gentle hands put fresh, clean straw in the trough.

Then a newborn baby was laid upon it.

Suddenly the first tree knew that it was holding the greatest treasure the world had ever known.

A shipwright took the wood from the second tree.

He sawed it and shaped it and smoothed it and sealed it.

Fishermen came and trundled it away. Each evening, they slid it onto the violet-blue waters of a lake, sailed off into the night, and cast their nets – later to haul them aboard full of slithering fish.

"Such a weary life," said the tree, "and among such ordinary people."

One night, storm winds blew and great waves crashed.

Then a man stood up in the boat and spoke to the storm: "Peace. Be still."

At once there was calm.

And the second tree knew that it was carrying the mightiest king the world had ever known.

The wood from the third tree was roughly hewn and left in a woodyard, almost forgotten.

Then one day came a clamour of voices.

"Any wood will do, but fetch it quickly."

Rough hands grasped the wood and hastily made a cross.

Cruel hands forced a man onto it and nailed him there by his hands and feet.

Soldiers hoisted the cross upright.

There, on a low, barren hilltop, the man died.

 The tree that became a cross was left empty.

As the sun sank low, it felt despair deeper than it had ever known. Though the sun rose and set again, every hour felt like darkness.

Then came a bright dawn. By a miracle, the man who had died
was seen alive again.

The tree that had borne his death was now a symbol of his life.

And the third tree knew that it would stand for ever, pointing
to heaven.

To Matt Ford and all other soldiers far from home—CF and TH

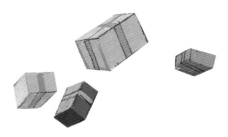

A GOLDEN BOOK · NEW YORK

Copyright © 2006 by Trish Holland and Christine Ford. Illustrations copyright © 2006 by John Manders. All rights reserved. Published in the United States by Golden Books, an imprint of Random House Children's Books, a division of Random House, Inc., New York. GOLDEN BOOKS, A GOLDEN BOOK, the G colophon, and the distinctive gold spine are registered trademarks of Random House, Inc.

ISBN-13: 978-0-375-83795-1

ISBN: 0-375-83795-7

www.goldenbooks.com

www.randomhouse.com/kids

Educators and librarians, for a variety of teaching tools, visit us at

www.randomhouse.com/teachers

Library of Congress Control Number: 2005932058

PRINTED IN CHINA

First Edition

10 9 8 7 6 5 4 3 2 1

The Soldiers' Night Before Christmas

By Trish Holland and Christine Ford

Illustrated by John Manders

A GOLDEN BOOK · NEW YORK

'Twas the night before Christmas, and all
    through the base
Only sentries were stirring—they guarded the place.

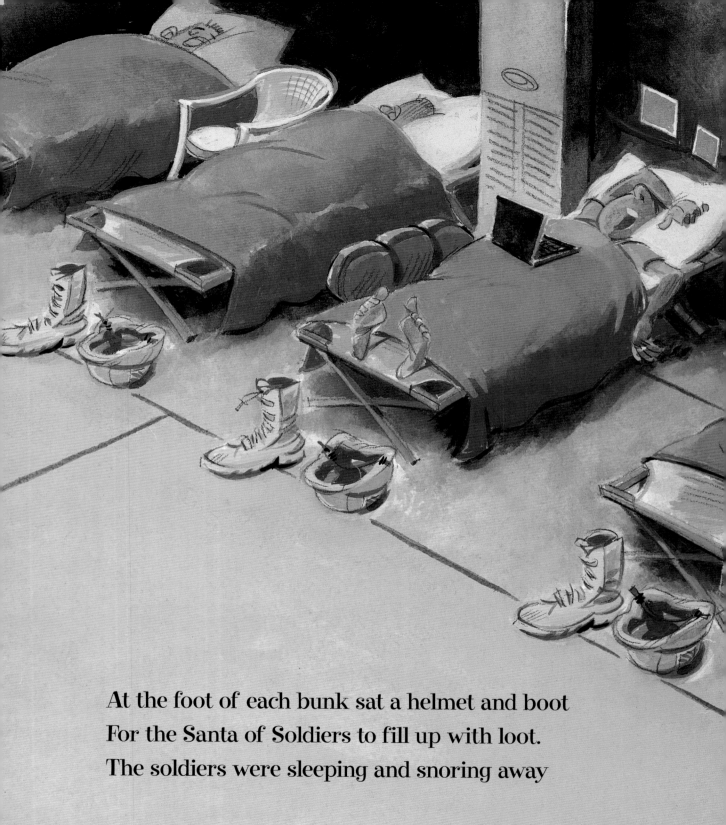

At the foot of each bunk sat a helmet and boot
For the Santa of Soldiers to fill up with loot.
The soldiers were sleeping and snoring away

As they dreamed of "back home" on
      good Christmas Day.
One snoozed with his rifle—he seemed so content.
I slept with the letters my family had sent.

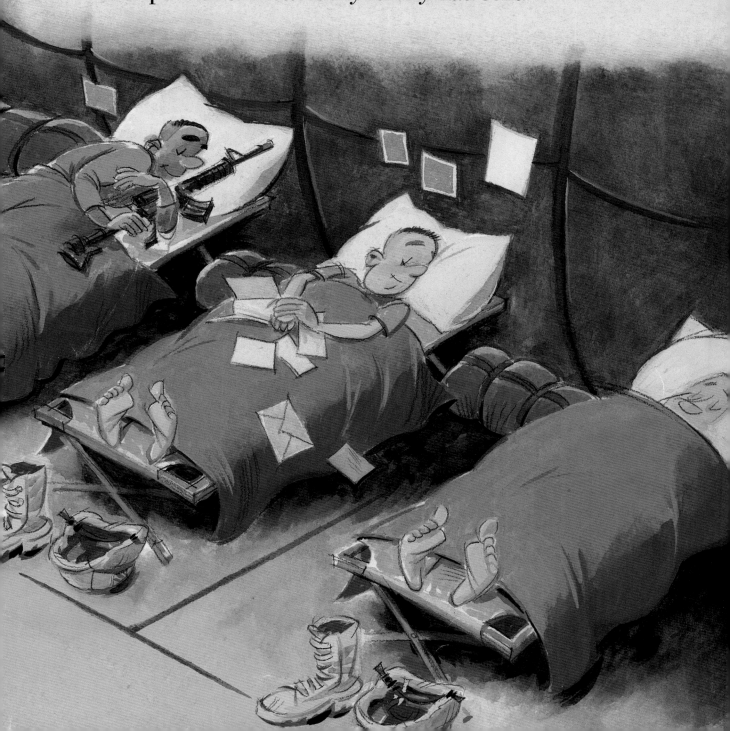

When outside the tent there arose such a clatter,
I sprang from my rack to see what was the matter.

Away to the window I flew like a flash,
Poked out my head, and yelled, "What was that crash?"

When what to my thrill and relief should appear,
But one of our Blackhawks to give the all clear.
More rattles and rumbles! I heard a deep whine!

Then up drove eight Humvees, a jeep close behind . . .
Each vehicle painted a bright Christmas green,
With more lights and gold tinsel than I'd ever seen.

The convoy commander leaped down and he paused.
I knew then and there it was Sergeant McClaus!
More rapid than rockets, his drivers they came
When he whistled, and shouted, and called
    them by name:
"Now, Cohen! Mendoza! Woslowski! McCord!
Now, Li! Watts! Donetti! And Specialist Ford!"

"Go fill up my sea bags with gifts large and small!
Now dash away! Dash away! Dash away, all!"
In the blink of an eye, to their trucks the troops darted.

The engines did flutter, they sputtered, then started.
The armored moved out—it was "Duty or bust."
McClaus disappeared in all of the dust!

As I drew in my head and was turning around,
Through the tent flap the sergeant came in with a bound.
He was dressed all in camo and looked quite a sight
With a Santa hat added for this special night.

His eyes—sharp as lasers! He stood six feet six.
His nose was quite crooked, his jaw hard as bricks!
A stub of cigar he held clamped in his teeth,
And the smoke, it encircled his head like a wreath.

A young driver walked in with a seabag in tow.
McClaus took the bag, told the driver to go.
Then the sarge went to work. And his mission today?
Bring Christmas from home to the troops far away!

Tasty gifts from old friends in the helmets he laid.
There were candies, and cookies, and cakes, all homemade.
Many parents sent phone cards so soldiers could hear
Treasured voices and laughter of those they held dear.

Loving husbands and wives had mailed photos galore
Of weddings and birthdays and first steps and more.
And for each soldier's boot, like a warm, happy hug,
There was art from the children at home sweet and snug.

As he finished the job—did I see a twinkle?
Was that a small smile or instead just a wrinkle?
To the top of his brow he raised up his hand
And gave a salute that made me feel grand.

I gasped in surprise when, his face all aglow,
He gave a huge grin and a big HO! HO! HO!

HO! HO! HO! from the barracks and then from the base.
HO! HO! HO! as the convoy sped up into space.

As the camp radar lost him, I heard this faint call:
"HAPPY CHRISTMAS,
BRAVE SOLDIERS!
MAY PEACE COME TO ALL!"

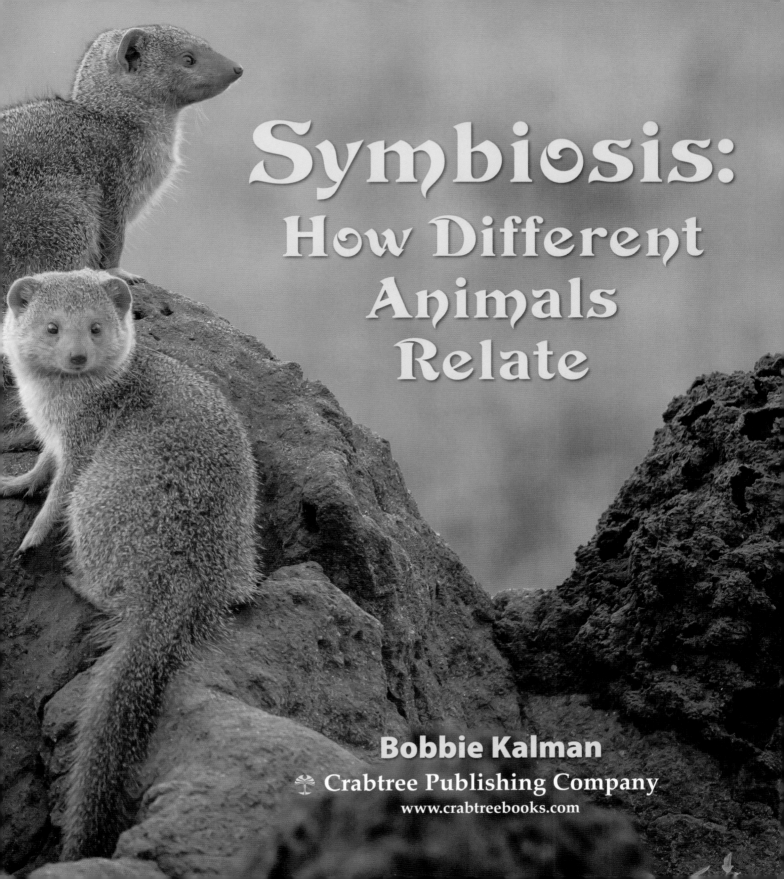

Symbiosis:
How Different Animals Relate

Bobbie Kalman

Crabtree Publishing Company
www.crabtreebooks.com

Big Science Ideas

Created by Bobbie Kalman

For our friend Donald George,
a kind and wonderful person and a fabulous artist

Author
Bobbie Kalman

Photo research
Bobbie Kalman

Editors
Kathy Middleton
Crystal Sikkens

Design
Bobbie Kalman
Katherine Berti

Print and production coordinator
Katherine Berti

Photographs
Dreamstime: page 23 (top left)
Istockphoto: page 22
Franco Volpato / Shutterstock.com:
  page 16 (bottom left)
Other images by Shutterstock

Library and Archives Canada Cataloguing in Publication

Kalman, Bobbie, author
    Symbiosis : how different animals relate / Bobbie Kalman.

(Big science ideas)
Includes index.
Issued in print and electronic formats.
ISBN 978-0-7787-2785-9 (bound).--ISBN 978-0-7787-2823-8 (paperback).--
ISBN 978-1-4271-8098-8 (html)

    1. Symbiosis--Juvenile literature. I. Title. II. Series: Kalman,
Bobbie. Big science ideas.

QH548.K35 2016   j577.8'5   C2015-908710-4
                                         C2015-908711-2

Library of Congress Cataloging-in-Publication Data

Names: Kalman, Bobbie, author.
Title: Symbiosis : how different animals relate / Bobbie Kalman.
Description: Crabtree Publishing Company, 2016. | Series: Big science
  ideas | Includes index. | Description based on print version record and
  CIP data provided by publisher; resource not viewed.
Identifiers: LCCN 2015046850 (print) | LCCN 2015044804 (ebook) |
  ISBN 9781427180988 (electronic HTML) | ISBN 9780778727859
  (reinforced library binding : alk. paper) | ISBN 9780778728238 (pbk. :
  alk. paper)
Subjects: LCSH: Symbiosis--Juvenile literature. | Mutualism
  (Biology)--Juvenile literature. | Animal behavior--Juvenile literature.
Classification: LCC QH548 (print) | LCC QH548 .K35 2016 (ebook) |
  DDC 577.8/5--dc23
LC record available at http://lccn.loc.gov/2015046850

Crabtree Publishing Company

Printed in Canada/022016/IH20151223

www.crabtreebooks.com   1-800-387-7650
Copyright © **2016 CRABTREE PUBLISHING COMPANY**. All rights reserved. No part of this publication may be reproduced, stored in a
retrieval system or be transmitted in any form or by any means, electronic, mechanical, photocopying, recording, or otherwise, without the prior
written permission of Crabtree Publishing Company. In Canada: We acknowledge the financial support of the Government of Canada through the
Canada Book Fund for our publishing activities.

Published in Canada
Crabtree Publishing
616 Welland Ave.
St. Catharines, Ontario
L2M 5V6

Published in the United States
Crabtree Publishing
PMB 59051
350 Fifth Avenue, 59th Floor
New York, New York 10118

Published in the United Kingdom
Crabtree Publishing
Maritime House
Basin Road North, Hove
BN41 1WR

Published in Australia
Crabtree Publishing
3 Charles Street
Coburg North
VIC 3058

Contents

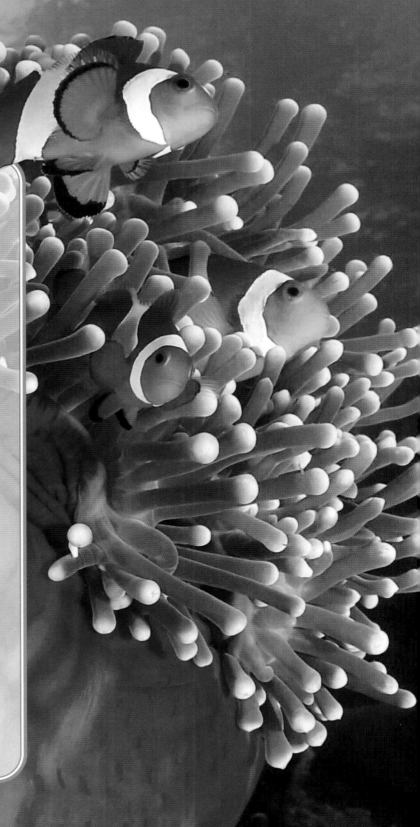

What is symbiosis?

Symbiosis is a difficult word, but it is an easy idea. It describes the close relationship of two different species of living things that help, harm, or have no effect on each other. This book is about the four main kinds of relationships that different animals have. Which of these relationships do you have with other people or animals?

ticks

Four symbiotic relationships

Mutualism
Both species benefit from their relationship.

Commensalism
One species benefits and does not help or hurt the other species.

Parasitism
One species benefits while harming another species.

Predation
One species, a **predator**, benefits by feeding on another, called its **prey**.

This impala and the dog on the opposite page both have ticks on their bodies. Ticks feed on the blood of these animals. The birds shown here, called oxpeckers, are looking for ticks to eat. Why does the impala allow the birds to sit on its head and back?

5

Animals that clean

A **parasite** such as a tick or flea lives on another living thing, called a host. Parasites often harm their host animals by feeding on their blood or taking other nutrients from their bodies. Some parasites even pass on diseases. The relationship between a parasite and an animal it harms is called parasitism. When another animal eats the parasites on a host's body, it is taking part in a helpful relationship called mutualism. The parasites are removed so they will no longer harm the host, and they feed the animals that remove them.

flea

These geese are eating the parasites on this cape buffalo's head as well as those that have come loose and fallen into the water.

These birds look like earrings as they clean the impala.

Monkeys often **groom**, or clean, one another by removing dead skin, insects, dirt, and twigs. They groom mainly to make friends. What kind of symbiosis is being shown here?

A gray heron is using a hippo's back as a platform for fishing. These birds also clean the ticks from hippos, so hippos do not seem to mind having these birds on their backs.

Coral reef cleaners

To get cleaned, coral reef animals go to **cleaning stations**, which are areas in the ocean where other fish called cleaners gather. Cleaner fish eat dead skin and the parasites that live on hosts. Getting cleaned helps keep these animals healthy, and it feeds the cleaners. What kind of symbiosis is this?

The mouth of this giant moray eel is being cleaned by a fish called a bluestreak cleaner wrasse. The eel is happy it is being cleaned.

cleaner wrasse

Dangerous mimics

Cleaner fish have stripes along their bodies. They also do a "dance" to let other fish know that they are cleaners. Some are not really cleaners, however. They look like cleaner fish but are actually cleaner **mimics**! Mimics imitate animals they resemble. The bluestriped fangblenny, shown below, pretends to be a cleaner. Instead of eating dead skin and parasites, however, this mimic takes bites out of the fish it pretends to be cleaning.

This bluestriped fangblenny is a mimic that can do serious damage to much bigger fish by eating their flesh! Name the symbiotic relationship between the fangblenny and the fish it pretends to clean.

Mutual survival

A sea anemone is a predator that lives in oceans. It has many stinging tentacles surrounding its mouth. It uses these long, flexible body parts to capture and sting prey such as fish and shrimp. Some ocean animals, such as butterflyfish, are not bothered by the sea anemone's stings and try to eat their tentacles. Clownfish, which have **adapted** to the stings, scare away these predators. In exchange, the sea anemone provides a safe home for the clownfish among its tentacles.

butterflyfish

stinging
tentacles

Clownfish help the anemone by cleaning it. The anemone also receives nutrients from clownfish waste.

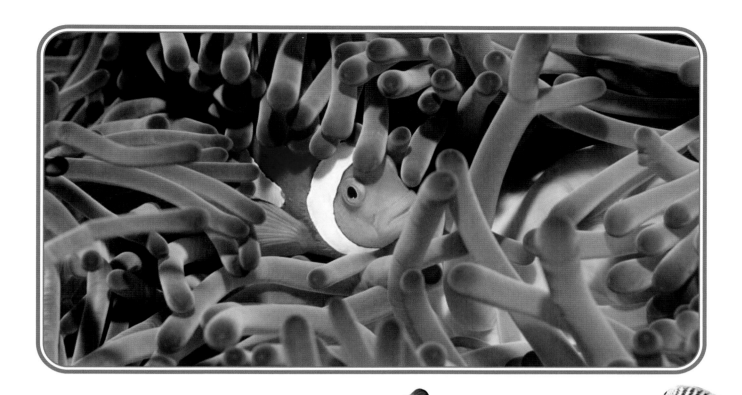

Help and protection

Clownfish and sea anemones protect one another from predators, as well as helping one another find food. Clownfish help anemones catch prey by attracting other fish close enough so the anemones can catch them. The clownfish then finish the leftovers. Clownfish also clean anemones and the water around them by eating their dead tentacles.

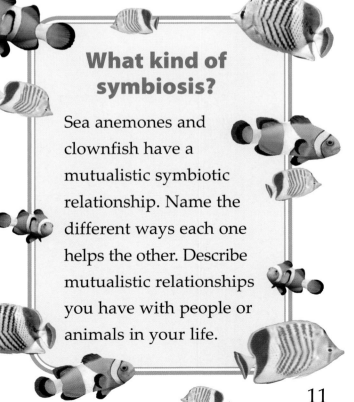

What kind of symbiosis?

Sea anemones and clownfish have a mutualistic symbiotic relationship. Name the different ways each one helps the other. Describe mutualistic relationships you have with people or animals in your life.

11

Help without harm

Two fish called remoras are riding on this sea turtle's back.

Commensalism occurs when one species benefits from its relationship with another without affecting its host. A commensal relationship is often between a larger species and a smaller one. The smaller species may obtain food, shelter, or a ride from the host species. The host is usually neither harmed nor helped.

These remoras are riding alongside this whale shark. They travel everywhere the shark goes and eat any food it does not finish. The shark gets no benefit, although some scientists feel the fish keep the shark clean. If this is true, how would this helpful act change this symbiotic relationship?

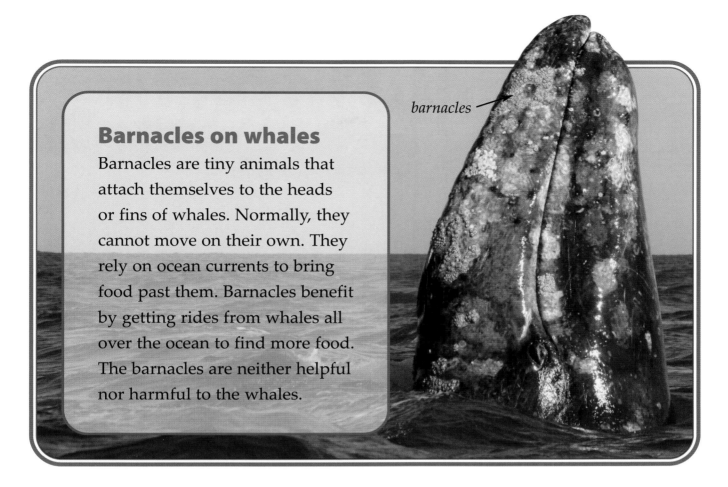

barnacles

Barnacles on whales

Barnacles are tiny animals that attach themselves to the heads or fins of whales. Normally, they cannot move on their own. They rely on ocean currents to bring food past them. Barnacles benefit by getting rides from whales all over the ocean to find more food. The barnacles are neither helpful nor harmful to the whales.

Hermit crabs often hide inside the shells of dead sea snails to protect themselves from predators. Why is this a commensal relationship?

What do you think?

Some people think that barnacles do not affect whales, but others feel that these animals slow whales down. Would slowing a whale down change the symbiosis between these two species of animals?

13

Helpful insects

Ants have developed a variety of symbiotic relationships with other insects. One of these is a mutualistic relationship with insects called aphids. Aphids get their food from plants. They use it to make a nectar called honeydew, which ants love. By stroking the backs of aphids with their antennae, ants can "milk" honeydew from them. In return, the ants protect and take good care of the aphids. They often move the aphids to areas on plants that contain the best sap so the aphids can make honeydew for the ants to enjoy.

aphids

ant

aphid

Ants sometimes clip the wings off aphids to stop them from flying away. Is it still mutualism when ants do this to aphids? Why or why not?

14

Pollinators

Pollen is the part of a flower that plants need to make fruit, seeds, and new plants. To make new plants, pollen has to move from one flower part to another part of the same kind of flower. Most flowers need **pollinators** to move their pollen. Pollinators are animals such as bees, wasps, and butterflies that visit flowers to get food. Honeybees pollinate many kinds of fruit trees, as well as vegetable plants. Their visits also help plants make the food that people eat. More than one-third of the food we eat depends on pollinators—especially honeybees.

What do you think?

Bees and plants help one another. Bees also help people by pollinating the foods we eat. People, however, have killed off many bees by using pesticides. What is our symbiotic relationship with bees?

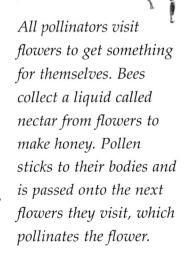

All pollinators visit flowers to get something for themselves. Bees collect a liquid called nectar from flowers to make honey. Pollen sticks to their bodies and is passed onto the next flowers they visit, which pollinates the flower.

Harmful insects

Malaria is a disease that makes people very sick. It is caused by a dangerous kind of parasite. The parasite is spread by female mosquitoes that have picked it up by drinking the blood of a person with malaria. The parasite mixes with the mosquito's saliva and passes into the blood of the next person bitten by the mosquito. Two weeks after a person is bitten, he or she will have symptoms of malaria such as fever, chills, headaches, and vomiting. Mosquitoes do not get sick from the parasite, but people can die of malaria.

These children live in Africa, where malaria spreads quickly. They are very sick. Malaria can be treated, but it often comes back.

What do you think?
How is the symbiotic relationship between mosquitoes and the parasite they carry different from the relationship the mosquitoes have with people?

16

Head lice

Head lice are tiny, wingless insects that live in human hair. They feed on small amounts of blood that they suck from a person's scalp. Having head lice is a common problem for kids because lice spread easily from child to child in schools. Lice make a person's head itchy, and they are hard to get rid of, but they do not spread disease.

*New kinds of "super lice" are now being found in children's hair. These lice are resistant to chemicals, so lice shampoos will not kill them. Using a fine-tooth comb is the best way to remove these head lice and their **nits**, or eggs.*

Deer ticks can bite people and cause them to become ill with Lyme disease. Do some research to learn which other insects and spiders are dangerous to people.

Parasitism among birds

Parasitism means that one animal benefits at the expense of another. **Brood parasitism** is practiced by most species of cuckoos and all cowbirds. Brood parasites do not have to spend time building nests of their own or raising chicks. They lay their eggs in the nests of other birds. These birds then raise the chicks as their own. Brood parasites such as cuckoos often remove and destroy some of the host bird's eggs.

cowbird chick

song sparrow

A cowbird laid eggs in a song sparrow's nest. The song sparrow is now feeding and caring for the cowbird's chicks.

This cuckoo bird is removing a reed warbler's egg so she can lay one of her own in the nest.

As soon as a young cuckoo hatches, it often throws the eggs of its host out of the nest. This newborn cuckoo chick is throwing a warbler's egg out of the nest.

The warbler feeds the cuckoo chick and raises it as its own.

What do you think?

Most cowbirds do not harm a host's eggs or chicks, but cuckoos usually do. Reed warblers must find a lot of food to feed the much larger cuckoo chicks. How are warbler mothers affected by the actions of cuckoos?

19

What is predation?

Predation is another symbiotic relationship in which species interact with one another. Predators are animals that hunt and eat other animals, known as prey. Predator-prey relationships are important in keeping **ecosystems** in balance. If predators did not exist, prey species could grow in numbers and eat most of the plants in an ecosystem. Other kinds of animals that also need plants to eat would starve.

Large animals such as deer, elk, and moose eat a lot of plants. When wolves eat large prey, fewer of these animals are left to eat the plants. Having fewer plant-eaters in an ecosystem helps other animals survive. Birds and rabbits, for example, depend on plants for food and shelter.

Is grazing predation?

Some scientists call **grazing** a form of predation. Grazing is eating grass and other plants that grow close to the ground. Cows and horses graze. Predators kill their prey, but grazing does not usually kill a field. The grass grows back, so there is no real damage to the plants. Do you feel that grazing is predation? Why or why not?

Are you a predator when you pick and eat vegetables or fruit? Explain your answer.

These horses are grazing on grass in a meadow. The grass they eat will grow back, so what kind of symbiotic relationship do you think they have with their food?

21

Nature's cleaners

Predators hunt and eat other animals. After they have eaten enough, part of their prey may be left behind. **Scavengers** eat these leftover parts of animals. When animals die, they still have energy and nutrients in their bodies, which can be used by other living things. Living things that eat dead things help clean the earth. The three main groups of "nature's cleaners" are scavengers, **detrivores**, and **decomposers**.

Scavengers include hyenas, jackals, vultures, and foxes. Scavengers benefit from having predators in their habitats. Is their relationship with predators an example of mutualism or commensalism?

Helping plants grow

Detrivores eat the remains of animals that scavengers don't eat, such as skin, hair, bones, and waste. Flies, maggots, cockroaches, and earthworms are detrivores. Decomposers break down dead things and clean the soil. Yeasts, molds, mushrooms, and bacteria are decomposers. Nature's cleaners feed themselves when they clean the earth. How do plants, animals, and people benefit from nature's cleaners?

maggots

Maggots and earthworms are detrivores that break down dead things that scavengers leave behind.

earthworm

mushrooms

bacteria

Mushrooms and bacteria break down dead things even more. The energy in dead things goes into the soil, where new plants grow.

Helpful bacteria

Sauerkraut is rich in healthy live bacteria, as well as vitamins B, A, E, and C.

Sourdough bread is another source of good bacteria.

Bacteria are tiny living things that are everywhere. They live in symbiotic relationships with plants, animals, and people. Your body is full of bacteria, both good and bad. Many kinds of bacteria make animals and people sick, but some are very helpful.

What are probiotics?

Probiotics are live bacteria that are good for your health. They are called "good" or "helpful" bacteria because they help keep your **gut** healthy by moving food through it quickly. Probiotics are found in your body, as well as in many foods. Which of the foods on these pages are your favorites?

One of the best probiotic foods is yogurt. Yogurts made from goat's milk are especially high in probiotics. Yogurts with added sugar and artificial ingredients are unhealthy choices. Make sure you read the labels!

Pickles made with sea salt and water instead of vinegar contain a lot of probiotics.

PROBIOTICS

Probiotics can be bought in pills, but many foods also contain them.

Some kinds of bacteria can make you very sick. Which two symbiotic relationships do bacteria have with people?

Miso soup has many nutrients and is high in probiotics. It is a favorite Japanese food.

Mongoose symbiosis

Termites are insects. Some termites build huge homes called mounds using a mixture of soil and saliva. Worker termites build and take care of a mound as long as their queen is alive. When she dies, the workers also die. What happens when there are no more termites in a mound?

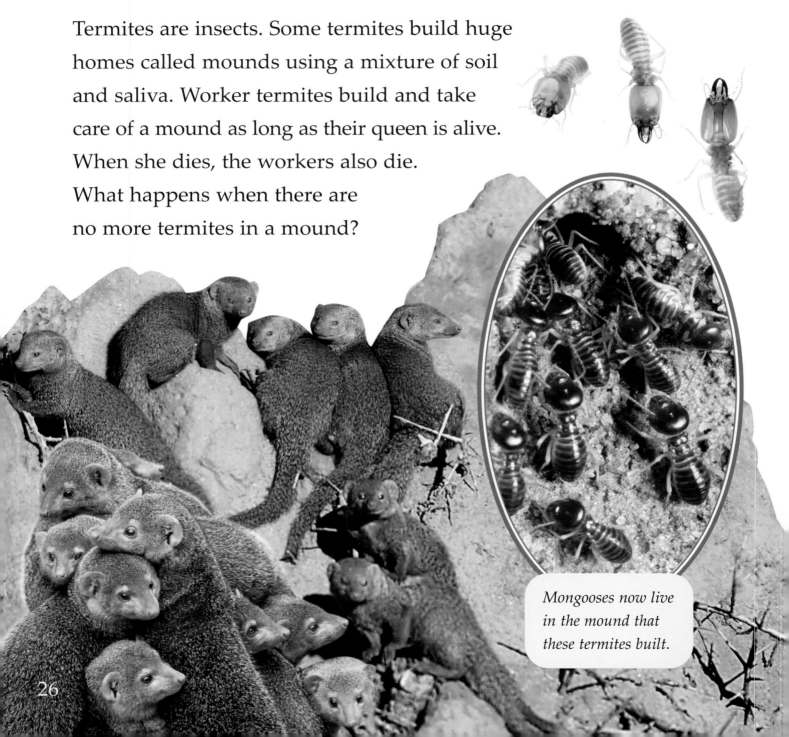

Mongooses now live in the mound that these termites built.

tawny eagle

jackal

Mongooses move in

A family group of 20 to 30 dwarf mongooses can live inside an unused termite mound. They sleep and hide inside and climb out to look for food. Dwarf mongooses are predators that hunt and eat beetles, spiders, snakes, and small mammals such as mice. They are also prey that are hunted by other predators. If a mongoose spots a predator, it gives an alarm call to let the rest of the family know that they must get inside the mound.

What do you think?
What kind of relationship do mongooses have with termites? Jackals and tawny eagles hunt and eat mongooses. What kind of relationship do they have with mongooses? How is it the same as the relationship mongooses have with the animals that they eat?

27

Mongooses, birds, lizards

Mongooses give different alarm calls for different kinds of predators. The calls tell the rest of the family what and where the danger is. Mongooses and birds called hornbills often look for food together. Both species warn each other of danger while feeding. Giant plated lizards also have a symbiotic relationship with mongooses.

Mongooses are predators as well as prey. See page 27 for which animals they eat and which animals hunt and eat them.

Mongooses share termite mounds with giant plated lizards and, in return, the lizards keep the mounds clean by eating the waste of the mongooses.

Mongooses have a different symbiotic relationship with birds called fork-tailed drongos than with hornbills. The fork-tailed drongo is also able to mimic the alarm calls of the mongoose, but for a very different reason. When it sees that a mongoose has caught some food, it lets out a loud cry, which sends the mongoose running for cover. The drongo then steals the mongoose's food.

fork-tailed drongo

hornbills

Which kind of symbiosis?

Mongooses have symbiotic relationships with many animals such as termites, jackals, hornbills, fork-tailed drongos, and giant plated lizards. Which relationships show:

1. mutualism
2. predation
3. commensalism
4. parasitism

Answers

1. hornbills, plated lizards
2. beetles, mice, snakes, jackals, eagles (See page 27.)
3. termites
4. fork-tailed drongos

What kind of symbiosis?

Name and describe the symbiotic relationships between the animals on these pages and then match them to similar human relationships in the chart on page 31. Write a story about your symbiotic relationships with animals or people.

A warbler mother bird is feeding a cuckoo chick and taking care of it as if it were her own.

The fish above is eating the parasites it finds in the mouth of the moray eel. By cleaning the eel, it feeds itself. Both animals benefit from their relationship.

This hermit crab is hiding inside the shell of a dead sea snail for protection. It did not hurt the sea snail.

Monkeys groom other animals to clean them and to be friendly. This cat is so relaxed that it has fallen asleep. What kind of symbiosis is this?

What kind of symbiosis does a fox have with a duckling or other small animal?

Name the symbioses

Which pairs of animals on these pages have these symbiotic relationships:
- mutualism
- commensalism
- predation
- parasitism

If you cannot remember, you can find the answers on pages 6, 7, 8, 10, 12, 13, 18, and 20.

Human connections

Which human relationships are similar to the ones on these pages? Discuss how they are the same and different:
- massage therapist
- bully at school
- dental hygienist
- adopted or foster child
- person living in an abandoned house

Glossary

Note: Some boldfaced words are defined where they appear in the book.

adapt To change in order to become better suited to the environment

ecosystem A community of living things that are connected to one another and to the surroundings in which they live

decomposer Organisms, such as bacteria and fungi, that break down dead plants and animals

detrivore A small animal that feeds on dead and decomposing plants and animals

graze To feed on grass or other plants that grow close to the ground

groom To clean another animal's fur

gut Stomach and digestive system

mimic To look or act like something else

nit The egg of a head louse or other parasitic insect

parasite A creature that feeds off a living plant or animal's body

pollinator Something that carries pollen from one flower to another

predator An animal that hunts and eats other animals

prey An animal that is hunted by a predator

scavenger An animal that feeds on dead animals after a predator has hunted them

species A group of closely related living things that can make babies together

Index